The Spark Files

Terry Deary trained as an actor before turning to writing full-time. He has many successful fiction and non-fiction children's books to his name, and is rarely out of the best-seller charts.

Barbara Allen trained and worked as a teacher and is now a full-time researcher for the Open University.

The Spark Files

Book Five

Dog Run

Illustrated by Philip Reeve

faber and faber

First published in 1999
by Faber and Faber Limited
3 Queen Square London WC1N 3AU

Printed in Italy

Cover design: Shireen Nathoo

A CIP record for this book
is available from the British Library

ISBN 0-571-19741-8

To my brother Roger and his wife Anne, with love.
Not forgetting their dog... Boozle. BA

Dog Run

FILE 1

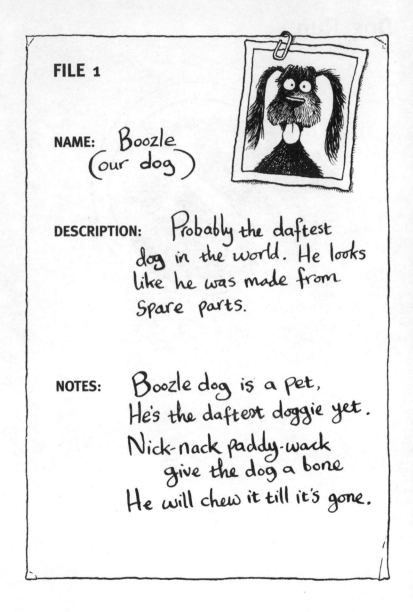

NAME: Boozle
(our dog)

DESCRIPTION: Probably the daftest dog in the world. He looks like he was made from spare parts.

NOTES: Boozle dog is a pet,
He's the daftest doggie yet.
Nick-nack paddy-wack
give the dog a bone
He will chew it till it's gone.

FILE 2

NAME: Sally Spark (me!)

DESCRIPTION: Without a doubt the cleverest girl in our school, our town, our country, our continent, the world and the universe. And modest with it.

NOTES:
Sally Spark is so good,
She'll end up in Hollywood
Nick-nack paddy-wack,
  give the dog a bone,
She has no faults, no
            not one.

FILE 3

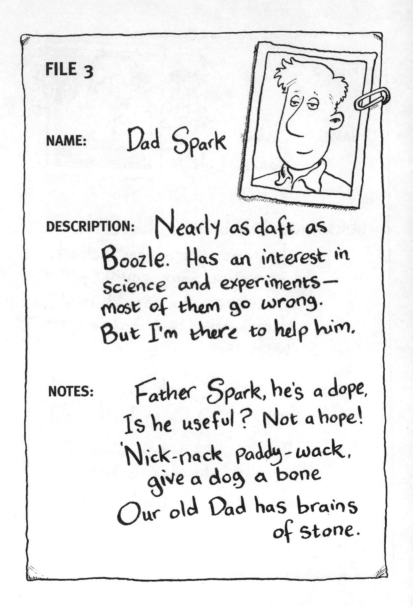

NAME: Dad Spark

DESCRIPTION: Nearly as daft as Boozle. Has an interest in science and experiments— most of them go wrong. But I'm there to help him.

NOTES: Father Spark, he's a dope, Is he useful? Not a hope! 'Nick-nack paddy-wack, give a dog a bone Our old Dad has brains of stone.

FILE 4

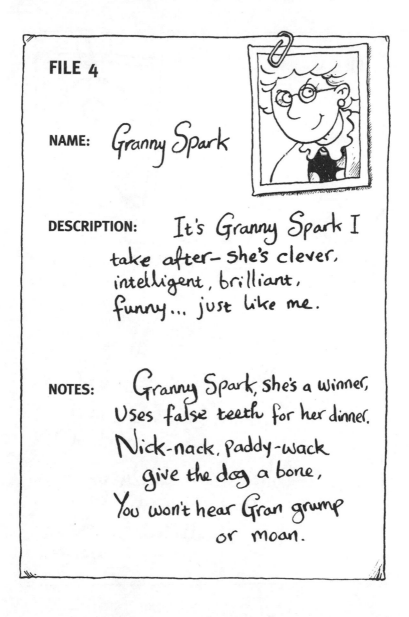

NAME: Granny Spark

DESCRIPTION: It's Granny Spark I take after - she's clever, intelligent, brilliant, funny... just like me.

NOTES: Granny Spark, she's a winner,
Uses false teeth for her dinner.
Nick-nack, paddy-wack
   give the dog a bone,
You won't hear Gran grump
      or moan.

FILE 5

NAME: Mabel Snook

DESCRIPTION: Well that would be telling, wouldn't it !!

NOTES: Mabel Snook is a bad'un
(Granny Spark she used to
madden)
Nick-nack paddy-wack,
give the dog a bone,
They should lock Snook up
alone.

Chapter 1

'That dog will have to go,' bellowed the mangled heap at the bottom of the stairs.

Dad had fallen over the dog – again – and crashed down the stairs. I keep telling my dad that he should *wake* up before he *gets* up.

'Why does that stupid, hairy, smelly creature have to sleep at the top of the stairs?' he shouted.

'But Simon doesn't sleep at the top of the stairs,' I said as I stepped carefully over my dad's crumpled body.

'I'm not talking about your brother. I'm talking about the dog.'

'He sleeps there because he is guarding us,' I explained.

'He sleeps there because he knows he can trip me up.' Dad staggered to his feet and crawled back up the stairs. 'I tell you that dog's dangerous. I'm going back to bed,' he said pathetically. 'Bring me a cup of tea, Sally.'

I was wondering why he couldn't make his own tea when Gran appeared from the sitting room.

'That's exactly what you need, son,' she said. 'A cup of tea cures everything.'

Gran was dressed in a floral pink dressing gown, fluffy purple slippers and a green tea cosy on her head.

'He's had a nasty shock. He needs a cup of hot sweet tea,' she said.

'He needs to open his eyes,' I muttered.

'He can't help it, Sally. His father was always falling over things first thing in the morning. It's in his blood.'

'I'm amazed he's got any blood left the amount of times he's fallen down the stairs,' I said.

'Mind the dog,' I shouted. Too late – Dad toppled over Boozle again.

Dad falls over Boozle most mornings. You'd think he'd remember that Boozle looks like a hairy black rug at the top of the stairs. But brains don't run in all our family. It's lucky that I, Sally Spark, am the cleverest person in my family. I am also sensible, beautiful and modest.

'Gran, why are you wearing a green tea cosy on your head?' I asked.

'I'm seeing if the colour suits me,' she answered and turned on the radio for the local news.

DOG WARDENS IN DUCKPOOL ARE ON FULL ALERT AFTER NEWS THAT A DANGEROUS DOG MAY BE IN THE AREA. THE NEW BREED OF DOG, CALLED POOXERS, WERE ORIGINALLY BRED IN EASTERN EUROPE AND HAVE ALREADY BEEN SEEN IN FRANCE. SOME FRENCH OWNERS HAVE ATTACKED AND BITTEN THEIR DOGS... SORRY, THAT SHOULD BE, SOME FRENCH OWNERS HAVE BEEN ATTACKED AND BITTEN BY THEIR DOGS. ANYONE WHO SEES ONE OF THESE DOGS IS ASKED TO NOTIFY THE POLICE OR THEIR LOCAL DOG WARDEN IMMEDIATELY.

'You can never be too careful when you get a dog,' said Gran knowingly. 'You need to know where they've come from. Some of them get all sorts of nasty habits from their parents.'

My revolting little brother Simon walked into the kitchen. He was digging into his right nostril with a grubby finger.

'Which parent did Simon get that habit from, Gran?' I asked.

Simon ducked as Gran leapt across the kitchen like a slug and swiped him with her tea-cosy hat.

My sister Susie, who is nearly as clever as me, walked in carrying a piece of paper.

'Simon, can I have a look at your science homework?' she asked. Simon and Susie are twins but you wouldn't know it to look at them. After all, one's a boy and one's a girl. And one's clever like me… and the other's called Simon.

Simon grovelled in his school bag which lay abandoned under the kitchen table and dragged out a mangled worksheet.

I grabbed the tattered paper and read it out.

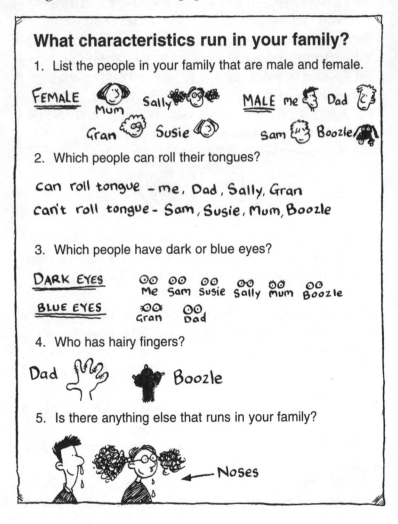

What characteristics run in your family?

1. List the people in your family that are male and female.

FEMALE   Mum   Sally   MALE   me   Dad
Gran   Susie   Sam   Boozle

2. Which people can roll their tongues?

can roll tongue – me, Dad, Sally, Gran
can't roll tongue – Sam, Susie, Mum, Boozle

3. Which people have dark or blue eyes?

DARK EYES   Me   Sam   Susie   Sally   Mum   Boozle

BLUE EYES   Gran   Dad

4. Who has hairy fingers?

Dad   Boozle

5. Is there anything else that runs in your family?

←— Noses

WHAT CHARACTERISTICS RUN IN YOUR FAMILY?

Dad limped into the kitchen, holding his back, and growled, 'Boozle's not one of the family.'

'Oh yes he is!' we all shouted.

'I'm going to sit down and try and recover from my broken leg. Will someone *please* bring me a cup of tea,' he whinged pathetically. 'And I might be able to manage a piece of toast.'

'I don't know what he's complaining about,' said Gran. 'When I were a lass, we used to fall down stairs for fun. In fact, we used to have "falling-down-stairs competitions".'

'Who was the winner, Gran?' Simon asked.

'The one who broke most bones. Ahh... those were the days. We may have been poor but we knew how to have a smashing time.'

We all groaned.

'I'll just go and check on your dad,' she added. 'I'm not having him lying around the house all day and making the place look untidy. I've got things to do.'

When she had left the kitchen we all crept to the sitting-room door to listen.

'You're not sitting there all day, you know,' we heard Gran say.

'But I'm ill. I've just fallen down stairs,' Dad moaned.

'You were asleep, you idiot. You don't hurt yourself when you are sleepwalking.'

'But I was sleep-falling... and it hurts.'

'Stop being pathetic and go out and do something useful. I thought Big Jim was coming round to play today.'

We heard Dad drag himself to his feet and in his firmest voice say, 'Mother, how many times do I have to tell you? I am a grown man, I do not go out to play any more.'

'I'm sorry, son, I forgot,' Gran replied. 'So what are you going to do this morning?'

'I'm going to my potting shed.'

The door opened and Dad strode out – not easy when you've got a broken leg!

'I'm off to sort my seeds,' he announced as he walked through the kitchen.

'Green fingers must run in our family as well,' Susie said, filling in her worksheet.

'I know how Simon gets a green finger... Yuk!' I said.

The radio crackled back into life.

HERE IS A DESCRIPTION OF THE DANGEROUS DOG THE POLICE ARE LOOKING FOR. IT IS A LARGE, GANGLY ANIMAL WITH LONG, FLOPPY EARS, A ROUGH, DARK COAT, A FRINGE OF HAIRS COVERING ITS EYES AND A STUMPY TAIL.

Susie and I looked at each other and said together, 'It's Boozle!'

IT'S BOOZLE!

Chapter 2

'Susie, can you remember where Dad bought Boozle from?' I whispered.

'No. I just woke up one morning and Boozle was here. Sleeping on this table.' She pointed to the kitchen table that was always covered in huge paw prints.

'Look,' I said. 'We are the only ones who have heard the description of the dangerous dog. So we must keep that information from the rest of the family – we don't want them to worry.'

'Yeah, and Dad keeps saying he's going to get rid of Boozle.'

'Let's go up the garden and talk to Dad. We'll pretend to be interested in his vegetables and see if we can find out more about Boozle,' Susie suggested.

It's good to have an intelligent sister. It makes up for the two stupid brothers I've got.

We found Dad in the greenhouse, fast asleep on a deckchair. He looked so peaceful that we decided to leave him alone and have a look in the potting shed. He keeps some of his important paperwork in there. The shed was full of old pots, seed packets, and lots of bits of paper.

But what hit us most was the smell – it was disgusting. It was a cross between manure, old socks and wet nappies … and it was coming from a dustbin in the corner.

'Do you think that's one of Dad's experiments?' Susie asked. One thing that does run in our family is an interest in science. Unfortunately Dad doesn't always get things quite right!

'If it is, I think it's gone horribly wrong,' I answered. 'We must leave it alone because it could be dangerous to take the lid off.'

'It's pretty dangerous with the lid *on*!' Susie said.

On the inside of the shed door was a poster for the horticultural show. Everyone called it the 'Cabbage Club' but they couldn't really put that on the posters!

DUCKPOOL ANNUAL
HORTICULTURAL SHOW

*DON'T MISS THE GREATEST
SHOW OF THE YEAR*

**CRAZY COMPETITIONS!
STUNNING STALLS!
FABULOUS FOOD!
POTTY PRIZES!
RIOTOUS RIDES!**

FUN FOR ALL THE FAMILY
PLUS
**FOR THE FIRST TIME EVER
IN DUCKPOOL:**

A NEW BREED OF FLOWER!

I wondered what Dad was up to. He had never shown any interest in gardening before. He only used the potting shed so he could hide from Gran.

'Let's see if any of these papers tell us what the experiment is,' I suggested.

We were so busy rummaging through the papers that we didn't hear Dad come into the shed.

His voice was slow and very cross, 'WHAT... do... you... two... think... you... are... doing?'

I turned round very slowly and looked at Dad. His face was purple with fury. This was not the time to make jokes about him looking like a ripe plum.

'Umm, we were trying to find out what was in the smelly dustbin in the corner.' I stammered. 'But we know we're not allowed to disturb any experiments. So we were looking for your design.'

Dad immediately looked calmer and his face changed to its usual pale donkey grey.

'Oh, that's all right, then,' he said, taking a deep breath. 'The dustbin contains my secret fertiliser mixture. It will make my vegetables grow huge and then I can win the prize for the biggest marrow at the Cabbage Club.'

'But, Dad, you aren't growing any marrows,' I pointed out.

'Ah, you spotted that? Hmm, that's the flaw in my plan.'

'What plan?' we both asked. Things were suddenly looking interesting.

'If I tell you, then you must promise never to tell anyone,' he said mysteriously.

'I won't even tell Gran,' said Susie.

'Especially don't tell Gran. She wasn't called the "Duckpool Grapevine" at school because she grew grapes. Your gran can't keep quiet about anything.'

'Go on, Dad,' I said. 'We won't tell anyone about your plan.'

Dad explained that he was not really growing huge vegetables. Big Jim had asked him to join the Cabbage Club because the committee was suspicious about a member who claimed to have bred a new flower. They called him in to find out what was going on. But they didn't want anyone to know, so he had to pretend to be a member. That's why he was making his own fertiliser. And that's why he had to sit in the greenhouse because his shed stunk.

'But why were the committee suspicious about the new flower?' I asked.

'Let's see if you can work that out for yourselves,' Dad said. 'Go and collect some different flowers from the garden and count their petals. You can record your results on a piece of paper.'

In the back garden we found six different flowers and took them into the shed. We counted all the petals on to the bench very carefully and this is what we found.

flower	number of petals
buttercup	5
lily	3
~~delf~~ delphinium	8
daisy	34
aster	21
marigold	13

We put the numbers in order and were amazed at what we found. You try it and see.

When you put the number of petals in order you get:

$$3, 5, 8, 13, 21, 34$$

But $3 + 5 = 8$
and $5 + 8 = 13$
and $8 + 13 = 21$
and $13 + 21 = 34$.

'What do you think about that?' Dad asked.

'I reckon that flowers can do maths,' Susie replied.

'The number of flower petals is nearly always in this 3, 5, 8, 13, 21, 34 pattern,' Dad said.

'But that doesn't answer the question about the people cheating with the flowers,' I interrupted.

'You're right. Now look at this flower that someone claimed was a new sort of marigold that they had grown.'

Dad put the marigold on the bench and we counted the petals. There were 10! It had the wrong number of petals so it couldn't be a new breed. Someone was lying. And our dad had been called in to investigate.

'Does this mean that you are a spy?' Susie asked.

'Sort of.'

'Don't start eating Polos then,' I suggested.

'Why not?'

'Because then you'd be a mint spy!'

We heard Gran shouting for us from the back door.

'We'd better go, Dad, before she gets curious,' I said.

As Susie and I walked to the house a thought suddenly struck me. We had forgotten to ask Dad about where he got Boozle. But we *had* found out that he was a spy!

Chapter 3

Susie and I were very worried about Boozle. What if people thought he was a dangerous dog? Would the police come and take him away? How would we save him? What we had to do was disguise him in some way. As the day dragged on the strain of it all got too much for both of us. We decided to tell Gran about Boozle. As we walked into the sitting room we heard…

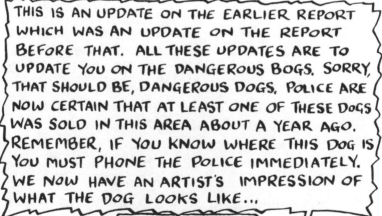

THIS IS AN UPDATE ON THE EARLIER REPORT WHICH WAS AN UPDATE ON THE REPORT BEFORE THAT. ALL THESE UPDATES ARE TO UPDATE YOU ON THE DANGEROUS BOGS. SORRY, THAT SHOULD BE, DANGEROUS DOGS. POLICE ARE NOW CERTAIN THAT AT LEAST ONE OF THESE DOGS WAS SOLD IN THIS AREA ABOUT A YEAR AGO. REMEMBER, IF YOU KNOW WHERE THIS DOG IS YOU MUST PHONE THE POLICE IMMEDIATELY. WE NOW HAVE AN ARTIST'S IMPRESSION OF WHAT THE DOG LOOKS LIKE…

Gran looked up from her knitting and asked, 'What's Boozle doing on telly?'

'That's not Boozle. It's a dangerous dog that the police are looking for,' I stammered.

'Well it still looks like Boozle to me.'

Susie and I watched her and waited for the penny to drop. It dropped with a clatter of false teeth.

'People are going to think Boozle is a dangerous dog.'

'Yes, Gran.'

'And they are going to come and take him away.'

'Yes Gran.'

'And we'll never see him again.'

'Yes, Gran.

'We must hide him.'

'Brilliant idea, Gran!'

But where were we going to hide the dog that everyone in the area was looking for?

'You girls get on with your homework while I have a think,' said Gran and closed her eyes. She would be asleep within seconds so there was no point trying to talk to her. Anyway I had some science homework to finish.

I found my science book and read the question. 'What can you find out about Charles Darwin? Write about him in no more than 170 words.'

I don't know about you, but my teachers ask some really stupid questions. I answer the questions just to keep them happy. Mind you, I can't remember seeing any of them smile. Perhaps they haven't got any teeth. I'll have a good look at my teachers' teeth if you'll have a look at yours.

I took my science book up to my bedroom, switched on the computer and searched for Charles Darwin. It didn't take me long to find something interesting.

CHARLES DARWIN 1809–1882

Charles Darwin was interested in natural history from a very young age. When he was a child he had collections of stones, beetles and biscuits. He went on a journey around South America to the *Galapagos Islands* on a ship called the *Beagle*. After his trip he came up with the idea of **natural selection**. This means that the animals and plants that survive in an area are the ones that suit it best. For example, plants that can survive without water are best suited to live in deserts. His idea was known as the **Survival of the Fittest**.

Recently some tortoises had to be moved from one of the Galapagos islands because of an erupting volcano. The tortoises are so old that some of them may have even met Charles Darwin. Some tortoises may have met him but some were made into soup and eaten by Darwin. Maybe he called this idea the **Survival of the Thinnest**.

When I'd finished, Gran and Susie were in the kitchen.

'Well, Gran, what are we going to do?' I asked.

'It's simple,' she said. 'You hide a book in a library. And you hide a tree in a forest. So we hide a dog— '

'With other dogs,' I interrupted.

But where would we find lots of dogs? At the grey-hound races – but there was no way we could disguise

Boozle as a greyhound. At a dog show – but no one would believe Boozle was a show dog – a show-off dog, maybe. We needed a place where there were a lot of dogs of different breeds. And it had to be with someone we knew would protect Boozle.

'I know,' I shouted. 'Myrtle Brick's granny owns a dogs' boarding kennels. She looks after lots of different dogs.'

'Brilliant, Sally. And no one will get past Granny Brick – or 'Crusher' as I knew her at school,' said Gran. 'Susie, you phone Myrtle and we'll take Boozle over there after tea. But don't tell him he's going to a kennels. I don't want him to be upset.'

'He won't understand, Gran. He barely knows his name,' I explained.

'He'll sense that something is happening. Our family has always had a sixth sense. We know when something is wrong. I know when something terrible's going to happen because my corns start to throb.'

'Well, I'm going to finish my maths drawings before we go,' I said.

'What do you mean "maths drawing"? In my day maths was sums and lots of them. The only thing we drew was the curtains. They're not teaching you proper maths at that school. I'll go down next week and have a word with them.' Gran was off again.

'It *is* proper maths, Gran. It's all about patterns. But I'm *drawing* the answers instead of just writing about them. I thought my teacher might like a change.'

'Let me see.' Gran snatched the sheet of paper from my hand. 'I still say it's not proper maths,' she said.

Patterns that are all around me.

The cycle of the moon—
every 28 days

The pattern made on the
sand by a sidewinder
snake

People have two legs—
mostly

Cats have 4 legs. Apart
from Flash, the cat that
lives next door.

Spiders have 8 legs, provided
my stinky brother doesn't
get hold of them.

Snowflakes— but only in winter.

Starfish.

Susie phoned Myrtle and arranged to take Boozle round to Granny Brick's kennels. We could relax at last. He would be safe. Or so we thought!

The front door crashed open and the boys burst into the room.

'Gran, Gran, the police and a dog warden are outside!' they shouted.

I looked out of the window. They were walking up our front path.

Chapter 4

GRRRRmmmmf!

BANG! BANG! BANG! The police officer knocked on our door. I dived for Boozle and clamped his jaws together. I didn't want him barking and giving the game away. Gran answered the door.

Gran shut the door and looked relieved.

'That was a close shave,' I said. 'I think we should get rid of Boozle as soon as we can. We can't wait until after tea.'

'But how are we going to get him to the k…e…n…n…e…l…s? Your dad has the car.'

'Why is Boozle going to the kennels?' asked Simon.

'Shhh, I don't want him to know where he's going,' Gran whispered.

Gran had a point about the car. But I had a plan. While I got the pram from the garage, Gran told the boys about the dangerous dogs. It took a lot of biscuits and half a packet of cheese to get Boozle into the pram. We tied a baby's bonnet round his head and tucked him in. He looked really sweet. Gran, Susie and I pushed the pram round to Granny Brick's kennels. We left the boys in charge of the house which was always a big mistake.

They were supposed to be tidying their bedroom, but didn't get very far before Simon asked,

'What do you think is the oddest thing about Boozle?'

'You mean apart from the way he looks,' said Sam. 'Yeah.'

'Well he sleeps in weird places... like in the airing cupboard and on the kitchen table and in nests of wet leaves... and he eats odd things like coal and manure and Dad's cooking.'

'Eating anything Dad's cooked is very dumb,' said Simon.

'And he chases a tail he hasn't got... and he howls at the moon... and he drools all the time even when there isn't any food around... and he falls over his own feet. But, apart from that, he's pretty normal,' said Sam.

'Mmmm. I'm off out for a while,' said Simon. 'Tell Gran I'll be home for tea.'

When we got home from settling Boozle in his run at the kennels I asked Gran, 'How do you end up

breeding a dangerous dog? Do you pick the dogs with really bad tempers and breed from them?'

'It's all to do with genetics and things running in families,' she answered. 'In this case dog families. I've got something about breeding cats in a book from when I were a lass. It must be similar with dogs.'

KITTY KAT'S COLUMN

Dear Kitty Kat,

I want a kitty with a really pretty coat.
How do I get one?

Kitty says:

You could just get your mummy to knit your kitty a coat. But that's just silly even for Kitty Kat. What you have to do is breed a cat with a pretty coat.

A really silly person might think that if you cross a black cat with a white cat, you would get a black and white cat.

What colour do you think the beautiful little kitties will be if you cross a black cat with a tabby cat?

Were you right? You will get all tabby cats.

If you cross two of these tabby cats, what colour do you think the pretty, sweet kitties will be?

Well surprise, surprise. You will get either a black kitty or a tabby kitty.

The reasons for this are very, very complicated. It's too hard even for most of your clever daddies to follow.

'So even if you bred from two bad-tempered dogs you couldn't be sure that you would get bad-tempered puppies,' I said.

'Puppies aren't born dangerous, my girl. It's people that make them that way. Let's see if there's any more on the telly about the dangerous dog.'

I turned on the television and we sat down.

WE HAVE MORE NEWS ABOUT HOW YOU MAY BE ABLE TO RECOGNISE THE DANGEROUS DOGS. THEY OFTEN HOWL AT A FULL MOON. EXPERTS THINK THAT THIS IS BECAUSE THEY HAVE BEEN BRED FROM WOLVES. SOME OF THEM BUILD NESTS TO SLEEP IN. IN THE WILD THEY USED TO MAKE NESTS FROM LEAVES. MOST OF THEM SLOBBER AND DROOL EVEN WHEN THERE IS NO FOOD AROUND.

POOCH PANIC

'It sounds *exactly* like Boozle,' I said. 'Gran we *must* find out where Dad bought Boozle. It may be the only way we can save him.'

Chapter 5

Suddenly we heard the back door crash open. We raced into the kitchen. Dad stood outside the door and was completely covered in mud. And he stunk. His blue eyes stared at us through the filth.

'Don't let him in,' Gran shouted. 'I'm not having him tramping mud all over me clean floors. Tell him to take his clothes off.'

I looked at Dad and waited... and grinned.

'It's not my fault that I'm covered in mud,' he grumbled. 'It was all quiet at the Cabbage Club until it was time to judge the best courgettes. I was terrified. It was like a battlefield with green torpedoes being hurled around the room. Then someone started chucking manure and mud.'

'Always getting into fights. Just like your father,' Gran said pointedly.

'I was trying to stop the fight,' Dad moaned.

'That's what your father used to say. Now get those clothes off and have a bath.' She handed Dad a towel and shut the door.

A few minutes later a miserable and bedraggled Dad walked through the kitchen towards the stairs.

'I'm not going to any more Women Only nights at the club. It's too violent,' he muttered. 'It's all been too much for one day. If that blasted dog trips me up again today then I'm going to get rid of him.'

'I think you'll be safe this evening,' I said sweetly.

The television evening news had another item about the dangerous dog. It was very difficult keeping all the news from Dad. After all, he'd be glad to see Boozle taken away.

I HAVE WITH ME TONIGHT MR GEORGE RUFF, A WELL-KNOWN LOCAL DOG EXPERT AND BREEDER OF BULLDOGS AND POODLES. WHAT DO YOU THINK ABOUT THIS DANGEROUS DOG THAT IS IN THE AREA?

I THINK IT'S A DISGRACE. DOG BREEDERS, LIKE ME, SPEND YEARS BREEDING GENTLE DOGS. I THINK IT'S NOT JUST THE DOG THAT SHOULD BE PUT TO SLEEP BUT THE BREEDER HIMSELF.

THAT'S A BIT EXTREME, ISN'T IT?

NOT AT ALL. IT'S TIME THE POLICE TOOK CHARGE. WE MUST GET RID OF THE DANGEROUS DOGS AND THE BAD DOG BREEDERS.

'Hang on a minute. Do you recognise that boy behind Mr Ruff?' I asked Susie, pointing to the television screen.

'Yeah, I've seen him about somewhere,' she replied.

Gran walked in carrying a blue stick of celery. She looked at the TV and frowned, 'I'm sure I know that man. I've seen him somewhere.'

'Perhaps you've seen him on the telly, Gran,' Susie suggested.

Gran smiled sweetly at her. Gran is at her most dangerous when she's smiling. I tried to distract her.

'Gran, why is that celery blue? Is it a new breed?' I asked.

'It's my way of brightening up salads,' she said. 'Come in the kitchen and I'll show you.'

What could she be up to this time? I knew she was writing a cookery series for the local magazine, but blue celery seemed mad. In the kitchen Gran handed me her latest article.

BRIGHTEN UP YOUR SALADS

You need celery (with the leaves on) and food colouring.

1. Put some water in a plastic drinking glass with five drops of food colouring.

2. Put the stick of celery in the glass.

3. In a day you will have blue celery.

4. Cut it up and put in your salad. Children will love it.

I wasn't too sure that I fancied blue celery. She'd be trying to feed us purple peas next.

The sudden loud knock at the front door made us all jump. We were used to Boozle telling us when someone was coming up the path. When Gran opened the door she was faced with two police officers. The female officer introduced herself.

'Good evening, madam,' she said. 'I am WPC Ningall. We would like a word with Mr Spark, please.'

'What's he been up to this time?' asked Gran. 'He's worse than the children. Sally, go and fetch your father from upstairs.'

Dad skulked down the stairs.

'Good evening, officers.'

'Mr Spark, are we right in thinking you were at the Cabbage Club tonight?'

'But tonight was Women Only night, officer,' answered Dad.

'We know that. I repeat the question. Were you at the Cabbage Club tonight?'

'Ummm, yes I was.'

'But how did you get in, Dad?' asked Susie. I really wished she hadn't asked that question.

'Is this your wig, Mr Spark?' asked the officer holding up a long, blonde wig.

'Not exactly,' he said cringing. 'I borrowed it.'

'And were you wearing it this evening?'

'Yes.'

'You were dressed as a woman, weren't you,' Gran shouted as she whacked Dad across the back with her handbag.

'Yes,' he whimpered, diving out of the front door.

'The shame of it,' Gran shouted. 'What will the neighbours say? It's a disgrace.'

'You have some explaining to do, Mr Spark. Would you like us to come in or would you prefer to talk to us down at the police station?'

Dad peered round from behind WPC Ningall. He cringed when he saw Gran circling her handbag round her head, ready for the next attack.

'I think I'd be safer down at the station.'

Dad was driven away from our house in a police car. Would we ever see him again?

Chapter 6

A cold east wind howled round the house and crept through the cracks in the floorboards. All night we stayed awake. It's terrible when a member of your family is locked up. We knew he would be missing us. Boozle wasn't used to sleeping away from home.

Everyone was very quiet at breakfast – except Gran.

'I'm going to kill him when he gets home. And I'm going to tell him exactly what I think of him.' Gran was still furious with Dad.

'But if you kill him then there's no point in shouting at him. A corpse isn't going to take any notice of you,' suggested Sam.

'You're too clever by half, my lad.'

'There'll be a perfectly simple explanation,' I suggested. I didn't want to tell Gran that Dad was a spy. A spy disguised as a woman.

Sam turned on the television for the local news.

HOW MANY OFFICERS HAVE BEEN TRAINED TO USE IT?

ONLY ONE, BUT WE ARE HOPING TO BUY LOTS MORE.

AND WHAT EXACTLY IS THIS LATEST EQUIPMENT?

A NEW BICYCLE. BUT IT'S GOT 36 GEARS AND IT'S VERY COMPLICATED.

FLEABAG FLAP

IF ANYONE SPOTS THE DOG — OR A POLICE OFFICER PEDALLING FURIOUSLY AFTER IT — WOULD THEY PLEASE PHONE THE POLICE.

'Sounds to me like they've lost the dog,' said Sam. 'There's a lot of places for it to hide down Sludge Lane.'

'I hope it gets away,' I said. 'Its owners must be really worried.'

We were interrupted by Dad's arrival. He didn't look like a criminal but Gran treated him like one. We kids all dived for cover in our bedrooms. It was over an hour before Gran calmed down. A dangerous dog is scary but a dangerous Gran is terrifying. Susie and I found Dad skulking in his potting shed looking worried.

'Don't worry about the police, Dad,' I said. 'It will all work out OK.'

'That's not what I'm worried about. Someone's been in my potting shed. They've moved all these bottles and jars around. I think someone at the Cabbage Club may know that I'm a spy.'

'You need to find out who moved the bottles,' Susie suggested.

'And how do you suggest I do that?' Dad asked.

'Fingerprints,' I said. 'I thought all spies knew that.'

'I haven't been doing the job very long. And I don't see how finding fingerprints will help.'

'Everyone's fingerprints are different. Once you've found some fingerprints all you have to do is find out who they belong to,' Susie explained.

She knew all about fingerprints from the project on classification she was doing at school.

'I'll go and print out the information from the computer,' she said.

'And *we* can look in this book.' I lifted a huge, dusty book down from the shelf.

DUSTING FOR FINGERPRINTS

Equipment: cocoa powder, small paintbrush, sticky tape, white paper

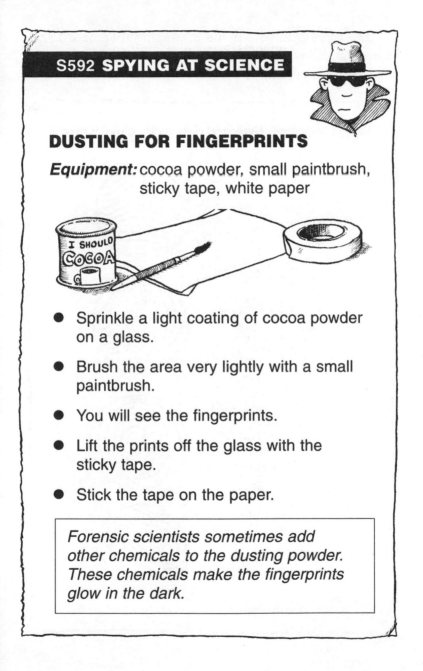

- Sprinkle a light coating of cocoa powder on a glass.

- Brush the area very lightly with a small paintbrush.

- You will see the fingerprints.

- Lift the prints off the glass with the sticky tape.

- Stick the tape on the paper.

Forensic scientists sometimes add other chemicals to the dusting powder. These chemicals make the fingerprints glow in the dark.

'Dad, I've printed out the information we need,' said Susie as she walked back into the shed. 'People have fingerprints that can be arches, loops or whorls.'

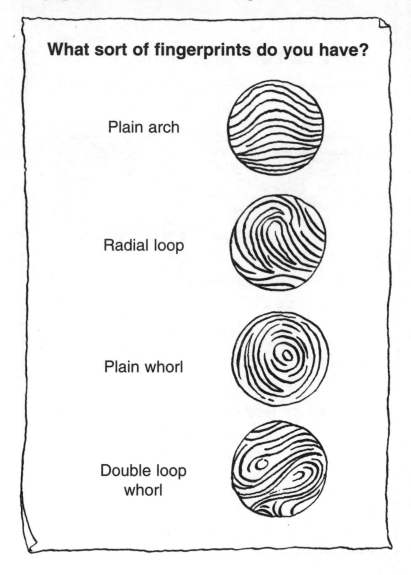

What sort of fingerprints do you have?

Plain arch

Radial loop

Plain whorl

Double loop whorl

All we needed to do was to take the fingerprints of all the family. Then we could compare those with the prints Dad had found on the bottles. The next stage was to find a suspect – a bit more tricky, but Dad had some ideas.

There was a knock on the shed door and Big Jim from the Cabbage Club walked in.

'We have a problem,' said Big Jim. 'Another one.'

Big Jim put a blue carnation on the workbench.

'That's pretty,' I said.

'It is, but you can't grow blue carnations. People have been trying to do it for years.'

Big Jim explained that the same woman who said she'd grown a new marigold was claiming that she had grown the blue carnation. And it just wasn't possible. But if she hadn't grown it, then why was it blue? An idea suddenly came into my head. I *knew* why the carnation was blue.

'Give me a day and I'll give you another blue carnation,' I said.

'You've got a bright daughter there,' said Big Jim.

'Brains run in the family.' Dad looked very proud.

'Big Jim,' said Susie. 'Why are you called Big Jim when you are only as tall as me?'

'Because I'm the tallest Jim in our family,' he answered.

'How many Jims are in your family?' she asked.

'Only me.'

We left Dad and Jim staring at the flower and went to pick a white carnation from the garden.

When I got back to the house Gran was on the phone. It sounded serious.

'Boozle has escaped from the kennels. A dachshund puppy was picking on him,' she explained. 'We can only hope he gets back here safely.'

'But, Gran, we heard on the TV that the police are chasing a dangerous dog. What if that dog is Boozle?' I asked.

'Right, you lot. Go and check all his usual hiding places,' ordered Gran. 'Let's hope we find him before the police do.'

BOOZLE!

Chapter 7

We hunted all morning for Boozle but couldn't find him anywhere. Susie and I had checked all the neighbours' sheds. The boys went down to the butcher's shop to see if he'd been in for a meat pie. Gran searched the house and listened to the radio to check whether the police had caught the dangerous dog.

Lunch was a miserable meal. Even Gran's blue celery couldn't brighten us up. Fortunately Dad didn't notice how quiet we all were. He was worried about the fake flowers.

'Sally, I need a hand in the shed,' he said mysteriously.

When we got to the shed Dad pointed to the bottles that had been moved.

'Don't forget we have to get fingerprints from *all* the family,' he said. 'But I don't want them to know why we're doing it.'

'Leave it up to me, Dad,' I said. 'I'll do it after tea but I will need your help.'

Back in the house Susie was listening to the radio. It was the local dog expert again.

'Boozle does that all the time. Do you think he really might be one of these dangerous dogs?' Susie asked.

'No chance, it's just a coincidence,' I said confidently. But even I was beginning to have my doubts.

Gran tiptoed into the sitting room with her finger to her lips. 'Come with me very quietly,' she said. 'I've found Boozle.'

We followed her into the garage where she gently opened the door of the tumble dryer. There was Boozle fast asleep in a nest of dry clothes. We could relax at last. He would be safe with us.

'I hope he wakes up soon,' said Gran. 'I've got some washing to dry.'

'He'll wake up when he's hungry,' I pointed out. 'And he has to eat every hour. So it won't be long.'

Tea was a much happier meal and Boozle was getting lots of treats. The trouble with Boozle is that he thinks he is human. If we let him he would sit at the table and eat off a plate. Sometimes I think I would prefer that to eating with my revolting brothers. But I had to be nice to them because I needed their help.

'Dad, you know I'm doing a maths and science project on pattern,' I said.

'Yes,' he said, but I knew he wasn't listening.

'I thought I'd do mine on fingerprints. They're patterns aren't they.'

Dad suddenly started to pay attention, 'That's a good idea Sally. Is there anything I can do to help?'

'Well I would like to take the fingerprints of *all* the family. I want to see if we've all got similar looking prints. I wondered if patterns of fingerprints run in families.'

'You get the things you need,' said Dad. 'You can do my fingerprints first.'

The boys thought fingerprints were great fun. They ended up with fingerprints on the paper… and on their faces… and on the walls! We even had to do Boozle's paw prints because he was feeling left out.

When Gran saw the state the boys were in she sent them upstairs for a bath. Boozle dived for the tumble dryer in case he had to have a bath as well.

Dad and I took the papers with the fingerprints out to the shed.

'We only needed to do my prints,' he said. 'Because no one else from the family comes out here.'

'I know, but I thought I'd *really* use them for my project,' I explained.

We looked at each bottle in turn and all the prints matched with Dad's. Until we got to a bottle of weed-killer. There were some different prints on it. All we had to do now was find a suspect and match the prints. But we didn't have to look far.

The prints on the weed-killer bottle were Simon's. What *was* he up to?

Chapter 8

The morning paper landed on the hall carpet with a thud. Dad's hand grabbed the paper at the same time that Boozle's teeth did.

'Oooowwwww!!!!! That stupid creature has bitten me. You can get diseases from bites.'

'I'm sure Boozle will be all right,' Gran said.

'I was talking about me getting a disease from him, you daft bat,' glowered Dad.

'I see Mr Grumpy got out of bed the wrong side this morning,' Gran said. 'Perhaps he should go back to bed until he can find Mr Happy.'

'I know one thing,' said Dad. 'That dog is dangerous.'

'Only when you fall over him,' I pointed out.

Boozle sat on the kitchen table and smiled. His teeth were glinting in the morning sun and the slobber flowed from lips. He was a happy dog.

The local paper was full of news of the dangerous dog – including the drawing that looked like Boozle. Apparently lots of people had been phoning the paper to see if their dogs were dangerous. So the editor of the paper had kindly included a questionnaire to fill in. I made the mistake of filling it in.

IS YOUR DOG
DANGEROUS?

1. Does your dog look like this? Yes

2. Does your dog drool even when there is no food around? Yes

3. Does your dog make nests to sleep in? Yes

4. Is your dog clumsy? Yes

5. Does your dog bite people? Yes

6. Does your dog howl at the moon? Yes

7. Does your dog prefer human food to dog food? Yes

If you have more Yes answers than No answers then we suggest you take your dog to a local dog expert to get it checked.

sponsored by **RUFF'S KENNELS**

It wasn't looking good for Boozle. But it didn't seem a very scientific set of questions to me. I reckoned that these questions would make a lot of owners get their dogs checked to see if they were dangerous.

'Do you think we should get Boozle checked?' asked Susie.

'No, I don't. But I think there's something odd going on here,' I answered.

'I suppose the dog expert would charge a fee for checking your dog.'

'A very good point, Susie,' I said.

Gran looked over my shoulder at the paper and pointed to a photograph on the front page.

'I was in school with her,' she announced. But we weren't interested.

'Yes, Gran.'

'She was always a badun.'

'Yes, Gran.'

'Cheated in her school exams.'

'Hmm.'

'But she copied from Crusher and *she* was even more stupid.'

'That's interesting, Gran.'

Susie and I had some talking to do – in private. In our bedroom we got ourselves organised. I had drawn the short straw and had to search the boys' bedroom to see if we could find out what Simon was up to. It was Susie's turn to take Boozle for a walk. She would have to take him somewhere quiet so that no one spotted him. So we put him in the pram again and she wheeled him away from the house.

The smell in the boys' bedroom was worse than a wet Boozle. Fortunately, it didn't take me long to find something suspicious. A piece of paper.

It was obviously some sort of coded message. And if Simon was using it then it had to be very simple. There were lots of codes on my computer.

A group of people called the Rosicrucians devised a simple but clever code. It was based on a system of grids.

To write using this code you leave out the letters and just draw part of the grid.

So the letter A is

The letter R is

And the letter X is

It only took me a few minutes to write the decoded message on a piece of paper. I slipped it in my pocket and went to answer a knock at the front door. The woman standing on the doorstep had long floppy hair, brown eyes and blood dripping from her hand.

'Your vicious dog has just bitten me. He's dangerous,' she announced.

'No he isn't!' shouted Susie as she panted up the path, pushing the pram. 'She put her hand in the pram but Boozle didn't bite her.'

'Then how did I get blood all over my hand?' the woman asked. 'I'm going to phone the police. That dog should be put to sleep!'

Chapter 9

'I'm sure I've seen that woman somewhere before,' I said as I shut the door.

'Who was that?' Gran shouted from the kitchen.

'A woman reckons that Boozle bit her. She's gone to phone the police,' Susie sniffed through her tears.

The newspaper was lying open on the kitchen table and staring up at me was the woman that Boozle had bitten – or not bitten.

'Gran. Who's this woman?' I asked.

'That's Mabel Snook. I was telling you earlier. I don't suppose she's changed.'

'Is it possible that she could be lying about Boozle biting her?' I asked.

'I'd be more surprised if she was telling the truth. Aye, once a badun always a badun.'

If Boozle hadn't bitten her, then what was the red stuff on Mabel Snook's hand? Was it blood? We needed to find out – and quickly – before the police arrived.

'Gran, when you do the washing, how do you check if a red stain is blood?' I asked.

'I use Hemastix. There's a box in the bathroom cabinet,' she answered.

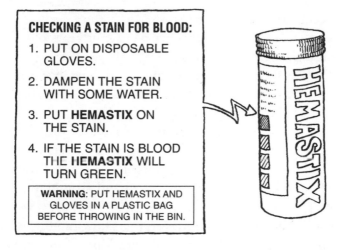

CHECKING A STAIN FOR BLOOD:

1. PUT ON DISPOSABLE GLOVES.

2. DAMPEN THE STAIN WITH SOME WATER.

3. PUT **HEMASTIX** ON THE STAIN.

4. IF THE STAIN IS BLOOD THE **HEMASTIX** WILL TURN GREEN.

WARNING: PUT HEMASTIX AND GLOVES IN A PLASTIC BAG BEFORE THROWING IN THE BIN.

I took the Hemastix outside and checked the stain left from the 'blood' on the doorstep. As I suspected it was not blood. It looked like tomato ketchup to me, but I knew that it could be dangerous to taste it. Unfortunately Boozle didn't know this. I went to get some cleaning things. But I didn't need them. By the time I got back, Boozle had licked up the red stain.

Soon afterwards, Mabel Snook arrived with WPC Ningall. But the evidence had been completely destroyed! This time Gran answered the door.

'Ah! Mabel Snook,' Gran said, glaring at the woman.

'Grapevine Gertie, as I live and breathe,' Mabel replied.

'Are you friends?' asked WPC Ningall.

'Never!' they said together.

'Been sworn enemies since we were four years old. She stole my elastic,' said Gran.

'That doesn't sound too serious,' said the police officer.

'It was holding up my knickers!'

'Can I help?' I asked.

I explained our side of the story to WPC Ningall, but Mabel kept going on about how she was viciously bitten by Boozle. And how she was going to be scarred for the rest of her life. She kept waving her hand around, but we couldn't get a good look at the bite.

'You should get that hand seen to,' said Gran helpfully. 'If you've really been bitten you'll need lots of injections. Wouldn't be surprised if the needle was so big it went straight through your arm and out the other side.'

Mabel went grey and started to stagger. I wasn't feeling too good myself.

'I think I'd better get Mabel to the hospital,' said WPC Ningall. 'I'll come back later. I have a few questions I want to ask you about your dog.'

Gran growled after Mabel as she walked away down the path. As I shut the door I remembered Simon's coded message. I hadn't told Susie about it.

'Susie. Upstairs. Now.'

We closed the bedroom door just in case the boys were eavesdropping. I told Susie about the coded message and showed her the piece of paper.

'I think it's time we had a word with Simple Simon,' I suggested. 'Let's go and find him.'

It's amazing how helpful a brother can be when you are sitting on his chest. He kept saying he couldn't breathe. But he must have been able to or he wouldn't have been able to speak. The coded message was to some

BOOZLE
SLEEPS
IN
TUMBLE
DRYER

new friend of his called Stinker. They were having a competition to see whose dog was the daftest. Well it's obvious that Boozle would win any Daft Dog competition. They had been sending each other messages for days and leaving them behind a brick in the school playground. It would have been a lot simpler to tell each other at school. But that's boys for you! Dafter than their dogs.

Before I got off his chest I said, 'I haven't heard you mention Stinker before.'

'New...kid...in...school,' he gasped. 'Staying...with... Auntie...Mum...in...hospital.'

'What's his auntie's name?'

'Auntie Mabel.'

Chapter 10

It was time to find out a bit more about Stinker's Auntie Mabel. Susie and I would have to think of a reason to go round to her house. Perhaps we could go with another message from Simple Simon to Stinker.

When Dad came home from another hard day's spying he mentioned the blue carnation.

'You said you could make a blue carnation,' he reminded me.

'Yeah, that was easy,' I said and raced upstairs to my bedroom.

Once we had the two blue carnations side by side Dad couldn't tell which was which.

'So how did you do it?' he asked.

'Same way Gran turned the celery blue. I just stood it in some water with blue food colouring in it. The water goes up the stem and into the petals. Simple. One blue carnation.'

'Two blue carnations!' said Susie.

'So the woman *was* cheating,' said Dad, 'but how are we going to prove it?'

'You haven't got this spying lark sorted out yet, have you? Use science,' I said pointedly.

'Yeah, Dad, you are a dope,' said Susie. 'All we've got to do is show that the food colouring used to dye each carnation is the same.'

'And how do we do that?' Dad asked.

'Chromatography,' we said together.
'Let's go and find your Spy Manual in the shed.'
In the shed I showed Dad the section on chromatography.

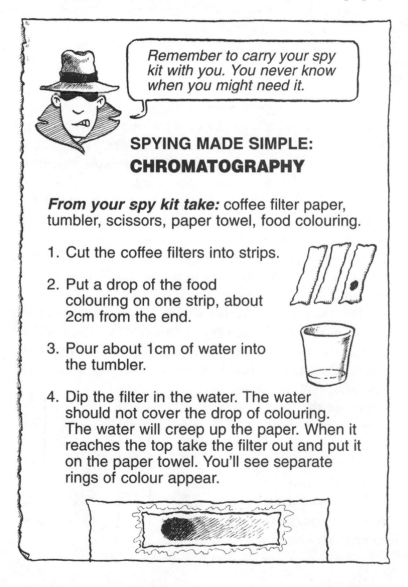

Remember to carry your spy kit with you. You never know when you might need it.

SPYING MADE SIMPLE:
CHROMATOGRAPHY

From your spy kit take: coffee filter paper, tumbler, scissors, paper towel, food colouring.

1. Cut the coffee filters into strips.

2. Put a drop of the food colouring on one strip, about 2cm from the end.

3. Pour about 1cm of water into the tumbler.

4. Dip the filter in the water. The water should not cover the drop of colouring. The water will creep up the paper. When it reaches the top take the filter out and put it on the paper towel. You'll see separate rings of colour appear.

'And what are you going to do?' Dad asked.

'We have to go and see someone,' answered Susie.

'By the way, what's the name of the woman that cheated with the carnation?'

'Mabel something,' Dad said.

'Mabel Snook?' I asked.

'Yes,' Dad replied.

This was all too much of a coincidence for me.

There was only one shop in Duckpool that sold food colourings. If we were right then the dye Stinker's auntie had used would be exactly the same as ours. Even though the carnations looked the same we had to prove that they had been dyed with the same colouring.

Susie and I raced round to Stinker's Auntie Mabel's. When Susie knocked on the front door I nipped round the back of the house to the shed. Susie was going to distract Auntie Mabel by asking about her bad hand. I could hear a dog barking in the house and hoped that Auntie Mabel wouldn't let it out into the garden.

The food colouring was sitting on the workbench in the shed. Perhaps Gran was right about Mabel Snook still being a badun. She hadn't even tried to hide the bottle of food colouring. Mabel may be a cheat, but what was more helpful to us was that she wasn't a very clever cheat.

At home we did the chromatography test on both the food colourings. The colourings were exactly the same.

'Well there's our proof,' I said to Dad.

'I'll go and phone Big Jim and tell him the news. Tomorrow we can go round to her house. She has a lot of explaining to do. The Cabbage Club committee will probably throw her out of the club.'

WPC Ningall kept her word and called round to have a word about Boozle. She went through the questionnaire that had been in the paper and was surprised when all the answers were 'Yes'.

'Why are you so surprised, WPC Ningall?' I asked.

'Usually people answer "No" to at least one of these questions,' she explained. 'It's as if the questions have been written to be a perfect match for Boozle.'

'What do you think we should do, WPC Ningall?' asked Gran.

'Please call me Eve. I can't stand being called WPC Ningall all the time.'

'Evening all,' said Simon as he walked into the room.

'How did you know the police officer's name?' asked Gran. 'And don't be so familiar, young feller me lad.'

'What?' Simon was completely confused and walked straight out again.

'I think Boozle is a poppet,' said Eve. Boozle was gazing up at Eve's hazel eyes. He was in love. 'But I think we need him checked by a local vet. You keep him indoors tonight and I'll be back tomorrow to get him looked at.'

I thought it was a good thing to get Boozle checked. At least then everyone would know that he wasn't dangerous.

The next morning WPC Ningall arrived early to take Boozle round to the vet. He was really excited at seeing his 'girlfriend' again and was jumping on and off the kitchen table.

'Where's that police officer taking Boozle?' Dad asked.

'They want to show him to some children as an example of a gentle, loving dog,' I lied.

'Mad dog more like,' Dad said.

'I'll bring him home as soon as I can,' whispered WPC Ningall as I let her out of the front door. 'I don't think it will take the vet long to see that he is normal. Well, sort of normal.'

Boozle trotted off leaving a trail of slobber. It was like a giant slug had slithered over the kitchen floor. In walked two more slugs. The two-legged kind.

'I'm going round to see Sniffer,' said Simon.

'Who's Sniffer?' Gran asked.

'Stinker's brother.'

'What revolting names.'

'Tell Gran who their Great Auntie is,' I said.

'Who is it?'

'Mabel Snook.'

'WHAT!!!'

I turned on the radio in an attempt to distract Gran.

'That's good, isn't it, Gran?' I suggested. 'They've found the dangerous dog.'

'Probably not dangerous at all,' she said. 'I expect the

owners treated it badly. It's the owners that should be put to sleep, not the dog.' She was off again.

'What!!' Susie shouted. 'The police have got Boozle. WPC Ningall lied to us!'

THE POLICE HAVE JUST ANNOUNCED THAT THE DANGEROUS DOG HAS BEEN FOUND. IT SEEMS HE WAS TAKEN TO MR GEORGE RUFF, THE LOCAL DOG EXPERT, BY A POLICE OFFICER. MR RUFF HAS CONFIRMED THAT THE DOG IS DANGEROUS. THE DOG WILL BE KEPT IN THE POLICE DOG-POUND UNTL HE CAN BE PUT TO SLEEP.

'Phone the television and I'll put the police on,' ordered Gran.

'I think she means phone the police and she'll put the telly on,' I explained to the boys. 'There might be more about Boozle on the local news.'

I was right. Mr Ruff was being interviewed outside the dog pound where Boozle was being kept. The dog expert was turning into a local celebrity – and he looked as if he was enjoying it. He went through the list of things that had been in the local paper. And explained how Boozle had also bitten a woman. All the evidence certainly made it look as if Boozle was a dangerous dog.

'That's all we need,' said Susie looking out of the front window. 'Mabel Snook is coming up the path.'

Chapter 11

'Sam, go and keep an eye on Gran,' I ordered. I can be really bossy sometimes – and it's fun. 'We don't want her starting a handbag fight with Auntie Mabel. I'll answer the door.'

I opened the door before Stinker's auntie had a chance to knock.

'I see your vicious dog has been locked up,' she gloated. 'In my opinion your whole family should be locked up. You are all as mad as your dog.'

'Did you just come here to insult us or did you want something?' I asked.

'I came to tell you that my doctor says I won't be able to look after myself for weeks. I'll have to get someone to look after me.' She said. 'And you are going to pay.'

'You can't get any money from us,' Susie said. 'The bite wasn't that bad.'

'Your mad dog is going to cost you a small fortune.' She shoved her arm under my nose. The bite looked nasty and painful. But there was something that wasn't quite right about it.

'I think you should go,' I said. 'We've got Gran tied up in the back garden but the chain won't hold her for ever.'

'She should have been tied up years ago.' Mabel Snook turned round briskly and strode off down the path.

'Come on, Susie, I know how we can save Boozle.'

'How are we going to do that?'

'With a polystyrene plate,' I said.

'I think it's going to take more than that.'

Susie and I grabbed our coats and some plates and raced down to the police station. When we got there we asked to see WPC Ningall.

'Please let us see Boozle,' I pleaded. 'I can prove that he did not bite that woman.'

WPC Ningall took us to the dog pound round at the back of the station.

'Now, Boozle, you must be sensible and co-operative,' I explained to the hairy, drooling lump of fur.

'Every dog's teeth are different.' I explained to Eve. 'Look at this impression of Boozle's teeth. I suggest you go and look at the bite on Mabel Snook's hand. It doesn't look anything like this. She must have been bitten by a different dog.'

'You go home,' said WPC Ningall. 'I'll go round to her house straight away. I never thought Boozle was dangerous. He's such a sweetie.'

It was really difficult waiting at home for news from WPC Ningall. Susie and I were helping Gran cook the meal when a hairy head with big floppy ears poked through the cat flap.

'Boozle!' we shouted. Outside the back door stood a bedraggled WPC Ningall. Her black tights were tattered and she had half a bush hanging from her shoulders.

'You look like you've been dragged through a hedge backwards,' said Gran.

'Forwards actually.'

'He must have taken his short cut I explained.

'Well I wish he'd taken his long cut. It would have been less painful.'

'GERROFF, you horrible smelly lump,' screeched Dad from the sitting room. He had been fast asleep in front of the telly. But no one sleeps in our house when Boozle's around.

'Someone get this stupid creature off me,' he shouted.

We ambled to the rescue. Boozle was sitting on Dad's lap with his front paws wrapped around his neck. The slobber was dripping on to Dad's chin. We tried not to laugh – and failed.

'He's missed you, Dad,' said Susie.

'Well I haven't missed him. It was lovely and quiet in the house when he was locked up.'

Susie and I dragged Boozle off Dad's lap. He struggled to his feet. I knew exactly how he felt. I feel the same way when I've been boozled.

When I turned round Gran was peering at the television. Dad looked over her shoulder and said, 'I know that man.'

George Ruff was being interviewed again about dangerous dogs.

'That's the man I bought Boozle from.'

Gran peered at the screen.

'But that's Mabel Snook's brother.'

We all stared at Gran in amazement. This was too much of a coincidence.

'Let's be scientific about this,' I suggested. 'We need to look at all the evidence. Then we might be able to piece it together like a jigsaw.'

'We do that down at the police station,' said Eve. 'But we stick all the pieces of evidence on a big white board. Then we can see if there is any pattern.'

'We haven't got a big white board but we have got a big white wall,' said Gran. 'In the kitchen, everyone.'

'Susie, cut up some paper into strips,' I ordered. 'My writing's the neatest.'

'What are you going to write?' she asked.

'The facts.'

'Well you can start by writing that Mabel Snook's a badun,' said Gran.

'I can't put that,' I said. 'It's not a fact.'

'Yes it is. I just told you it.'

'No, I mean it's not evidence.' I went on: 'You've got to write down stuff that actually happened not things that you think might have happened. Right, you lot. Tell me the facts. I'll write them down. The boys can stick them on the wall.'

We all stared blankly at the bits of paper on the wall.

'OK then, who reckons they know the solution?'
I asked.

Total silence. We didn't have a clue.

Chapter 12

We didn't know what to do next. It was lucky WPC Ningall was there.

'What we need to do is go through each fact and check that it's true,' she said.

'We know they all are,' I argued.

'But sometimes there is one that might not be.'

'Hang on a minute,' said Susie. 'Has anyone seen one of these dangerous dogs?'

'Not as far as I know,' answered Eve.

'Then can we be sure that there really is a dangerous dog in the area? After all, Mr Ruff is supposed to be a dog expert and he was wrong about Boozle.'

'I think we need to find out where the dangerous dog story originally came from,' said Eve. 'I'll make a few phone calls and see if I can find out.'

A few minutes later Eve came back into the sitting room.

'You're never going to believe who told the police that there was a dangerous dog in the area!' she said.

'Was it the French police?' asked Sam.

'You're not even close. It was George Ruff.'

We were stunned. Even Boozle looked stunned but then he usually did!

'The Sergeant has asked me to go and have a little chat with Mr Ruff. Would anyone like to come with me?' she asked.

We left the boys in charge of Boozle and the rest of us trailed behind WPC Ningall.

Mr Ruff was looking a bit nervous at the sight of a police officer on his doorstep. He looked terrified when Gran stepped out from behind her.

'We would like a word with you,' she said through gritted dentures.

As we walked into the sitting room we were greeted by a huge bulldog, a black standard poodle and Mabel Snook.

'Would you like to explain where you heard about the dangerous dog that is in the area?' asked WPC Ningall in a very official voice.

'I think I heard it on the television,' George Ruff said innocently.

'Then why do we have a record in the police log that you phoned to report a dangerous dog the day before it was reported on the television?' the WPC asked.

'Ah, well, mmm, yes, ah,' stammered Mr Ruff.

'Would this be your sister's dog?' asked WPC Ningall, pointing to the standard poodle. She seemed to have gone completely off the point. I was very confused.

'No, it's mine, but Mabel looks after it sometimes,' he answered.

'And would I be right in thinking that this is the dog that bit your sister?'

'Ah, well, mmm, ah, you know about that.'

'I know a lot of things, Mr Ruff. It's my job. And am I right in thinking that you once said in a television interview that any dog that bites a person should be immediately destroyed?' she continued.

'Umm, yes,' he gulped.

'Shall I phone the vet or will you?'

'No,' he cried. 'Not Trixie, she's all I've got. She's like a baby to me. Don't take her away.'

'If you would like to tell us the whole story I might be tempted to forget about the dog bite,' said WPC Ningall.

'That's blackmail,' I whispered in her ear.

'Possibly!' she whispered back.

Mr Ruff explained how his sister wanted to be famous for breeding a new type of flower. But she knew that if she did it properly it would take years and years of crossing one flower with another until she got what she wanted.

So she decided to cheat instead. But when our dad turned up at the Cabbage Club to investigate the cheating she knew that she had to do something. So she decided that Dad had to be distracted. If one of his family was under threat then he wouldn't be able to concentrate on his job. She convinced George to spread the story about the dangerous dog. And every day they gave a bit more information about Boozle's strange habits so that everyone would think he was the dangerous dog.

'But how did you find out about Boozle's habits?' asked WPC Ningall.

'I know that,' I said. 'They found out from Simon. He was sending coded messages to Mabel's nephew Stinker.'

'Oh no!' said Mr Ruff. 'She got little Stinker involved as well. She really is a badun.'

'I said that,' interrupted Gran. 'Didn't I? I said that.'

'She keeps dragging me into her schemes. And I'm sick of it. I'll do anything to help the police stop her.'

'Thank you, Mr Ruff,' said WPC Ningall, 'but I think the police have had enough help from you already.'

'But I bought Boozle from you,' said Dad. 'Where did he come from?'

'I was trying to create a new breed of dog. So I crossed Trixie with a bulldog and she had one puppy – Boozle,' explained Mr. Ruff. 'But he's so weird-looking that I'm not going to breed any more dogs.'

When we got home Boozle was racing around chasing his tail. Gran sent Dad out for fish and chips while Susie and I planned our revenge on Simple Simon.

'Will someone let that dog out before he destroys the house,' shouted Gran from the kitchen.

'He's just happy,' I said.

'Well let him be happy outside.'

I opened the front door and Boozle hurtled out and bounded round the front garden.

'Make sure the front gate is shut,' called Gran. 'We don't want him on the road in that mood.'

But I knew the front gate was open.

The squeal of car brakes cut through the air. The dull thud that followed could only mean one thing. A car crash.

'BOOZLE!' we all screamed and raced out of the front door.

Dad staggered out of the car. He was dripping blood from a gash on his forehead.

'Where's Boozle?' I asked. 'Did you hit him?'

'He raced out in front of me, the stupid animal.'

'But where is he?'

'WOOF!!'

He was sitting in the middle of the lawn, smiling.

'That dopey creature could have killed me. He's going to have to go. He's too dangerous.'

**Here is a list of the experiments in this book.
Have you tried them all?**

✳ Science Notes ✳